GW01057543

CAMMIE'S
(NOT-SO)
NORMAL MORNING

BY MICHELLE CHOINIERE

To Ginny,
thank you for sharing your puppy with me

First paperback edition August 2024

Paperback ISBN: 979-8-218-46756-2
Hardcover ISBN: 979-8-218-46758-6

Published by Michelle Choiniere

It was 9 o'clock in the morning,
and Cammie still hadn't been fed.

She had slept soundly last night,

wrapped in her soft blanket,

dreaming of castles made of food.

But as the sun started to rise,

she was ready to begin her day.

Morning time was Cammie's favorite part of the day. It would start with pats and scratches from mom.
Then, they would always go for a walk together.

Cammie would sniff everything:

the dirt,

the car,

the flowers,

the grass.

When they were done, mom would make breakfast. Cammie would get some food, and mom would get some food.

But mom's food was always better.

After breakfast, they would
snuggle together on the couch
before mom went to work.

But this morning was different.
Mom was late.

Cammie leapt from the couch,

did a *biiiig* stretch ...

and waited at the bottom of the stairs.

Maybe mom had slept through her alarm and needed help waking up? Cammie let out a small whine, but still no footsteps.

Maybe she needed to be **louder**?

She tried running

and jumping.

She tried rolling

and barking.

But no matter how loud she was, there were still no footsteps.

What if mom had gone to work already or left in a hurry to see her friends?

What if she had forgotten about Cammie and gone on vacation to Hawaii?

The house felt so big and empty.

Cammie's stomach felt big and empty too.

Oh, how hungry she felt!

grumble

grumble

grumble

She looked in her bowl, but there was no food.

She licked it just in case.

As she sniffed the floor for any sign of blueberries,
she thought she heard something.

Creak...

Cammie hurried back to the couch
and hid under her blanket.

What could it be?

Creeaak...

Again she heard it, coming from the top of the stairs.

Mom *was* home!

Cammie zoomed out from under her blanket and flew around the room. "Silly Cammie," Mom yawned, shaking her head. "It's Saturday!"

Mom put on her shoes and walked to the door. "Come on, let's go," she said.

Oh, what a beautiful day it was! Cammie stopped to sniff the pretty flowers. She rolled in the scratchy grass, and she just knew that mom would give her a big bowl of food when they went inside.

But Cammie's favorite part was that it was Saturday, and she could spend the whole day with mom, snuggled in the coziest blanket on the comfiest couch in the whole world.

Cammie is a miniature dachshund with a quirky personality. She enjoys blankets, blueberries, and popcorn. She loves her family and snuggling all day.

Cammie and her mom, Ginny

ABOUT THE AUTHOR

Michelle Choiniere is both the author and illustrator of this book. She is an ESL teacher at a high school in central Maine. She is married to her husband, Brad, who introduced her to Cammie (aka, the star of this book). Michelle has loved writing her whole life, and always dreamt of writing a book. However, it wasn't until she met Cammie that she felt she had a story worth telling. Writing this book has given Michelle the motivation to pursue writing in a more intentional way, as well as the confidence to continue illustrating.

Milton Keynes UK
Ingram Content Group UK Ltd.
UKHW052331280724
446164UK00003B/11